# JINGLE & SHAKE

## A FESTIVE BUS ADVENTURE



WRITTEN BY: BRET STEPHENS
EDITED BY: AMANDA STEPHENS

ISBN: 979-8-9896835-2-9

ONE FESTIVE BUS GOES
JINGLE AND SHAKE,
JINGLE AND SHAKE,
JINGLE AND SHAKE.

ONE FESTIVE BUS GOES
JINGLE AND SHAKE,
ALL THROUGH THE TOWN.

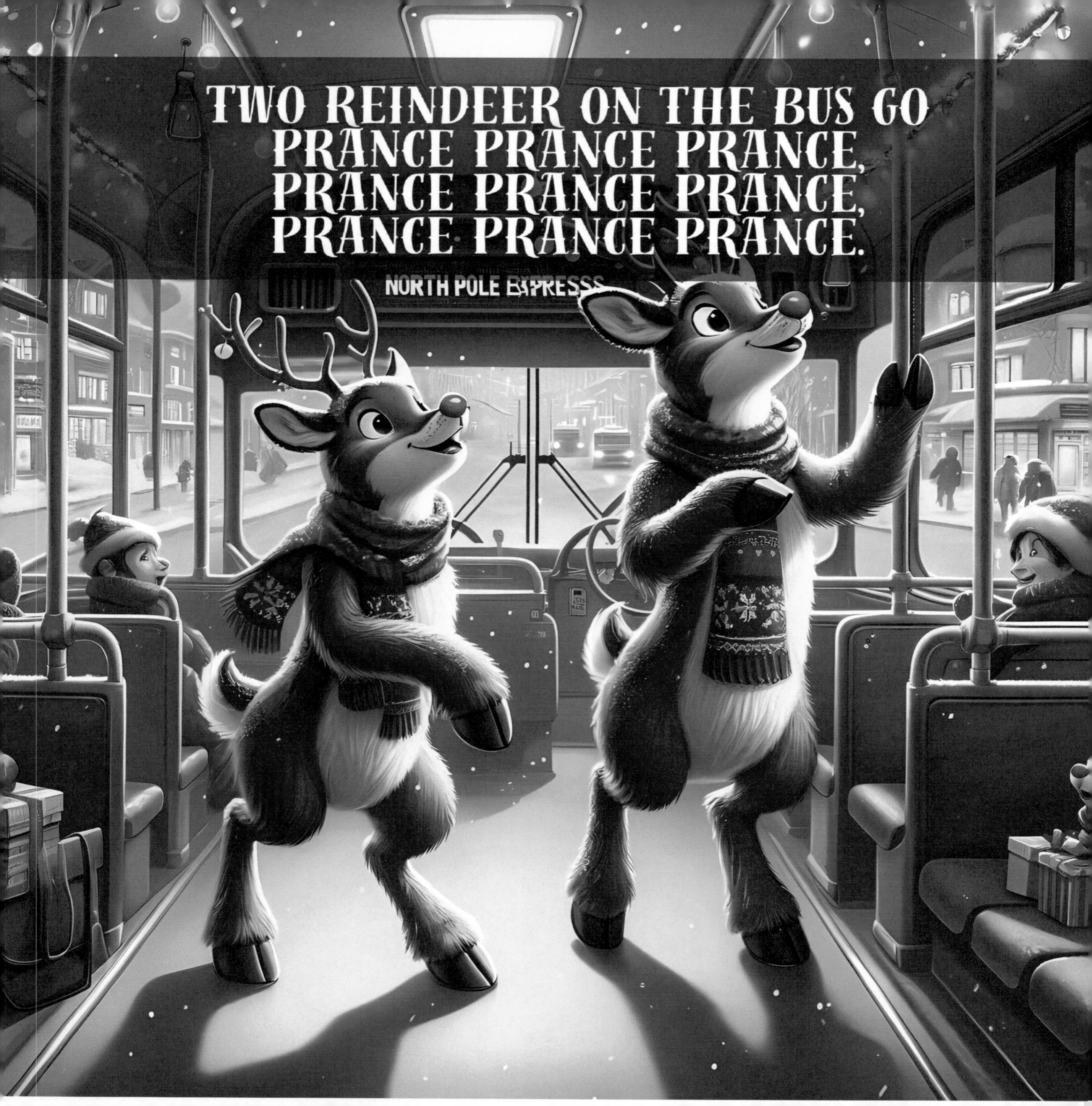
TWO REINDEER ON THE BUS GO
PRANCE PRANCE PRANCE,
PRANCE PRANCE PRANCE,
PRANCE PRANCE PRANCE.

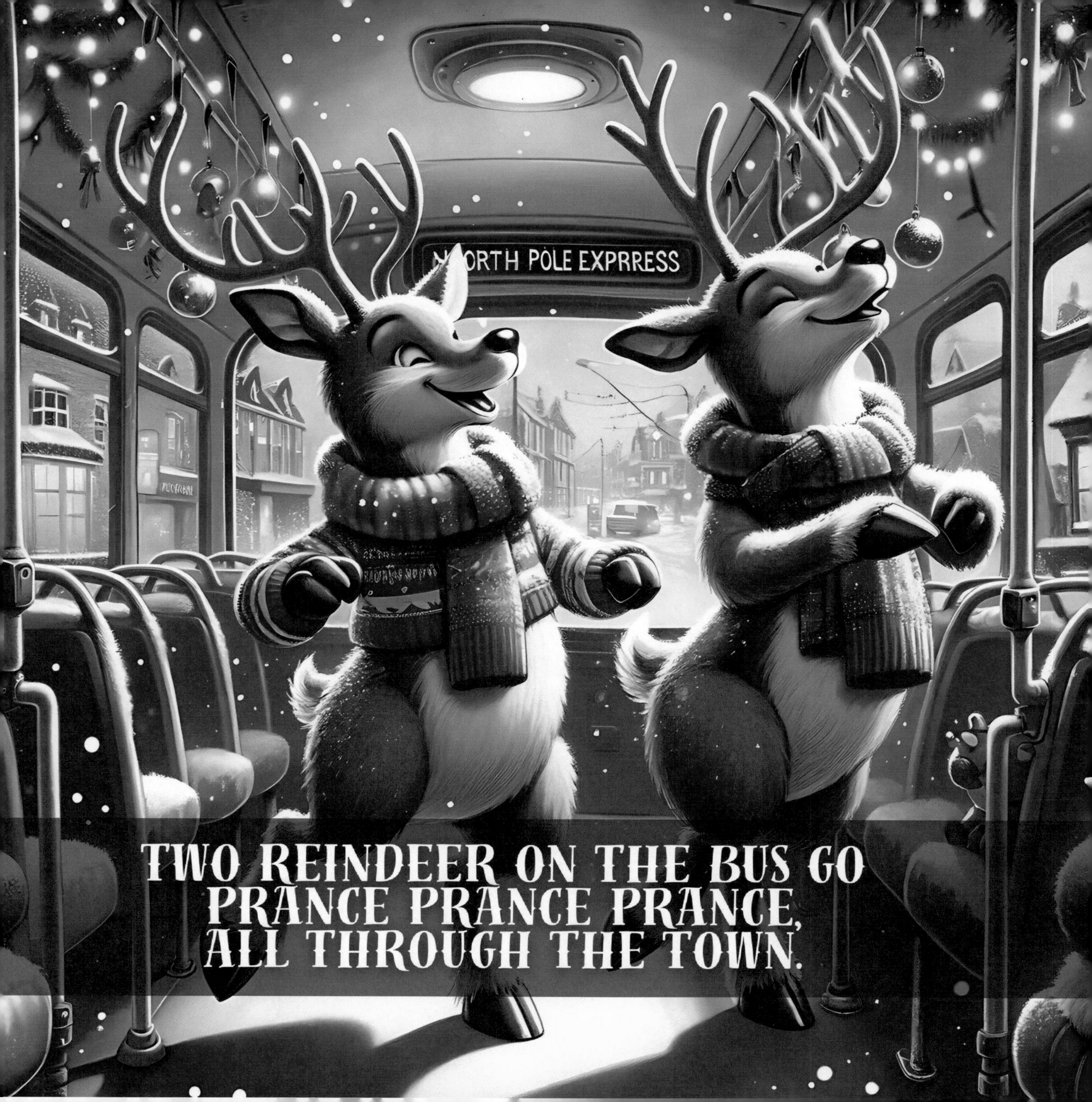


TWO REINDEER ON THE BUS GO
PRANCE PRANCE PRANCE,
ALL THROUGH THE TOWN.

THREE ELVES ON THE BUS GO
WRAP WRAP WRAP,
WRAP WRAP WRAP,
WRAP WRAP WRAP.

THREE ELVES ON THE BUS GO
WRAP WRAP WRAP,
ALL THROUGH THE TOWN.

FOUR STOCKINGS ON THE BUS HANG
SNUG SNUG SNUG,
SNUG SNUG SNUG,
SNUG SNUG SNUG.

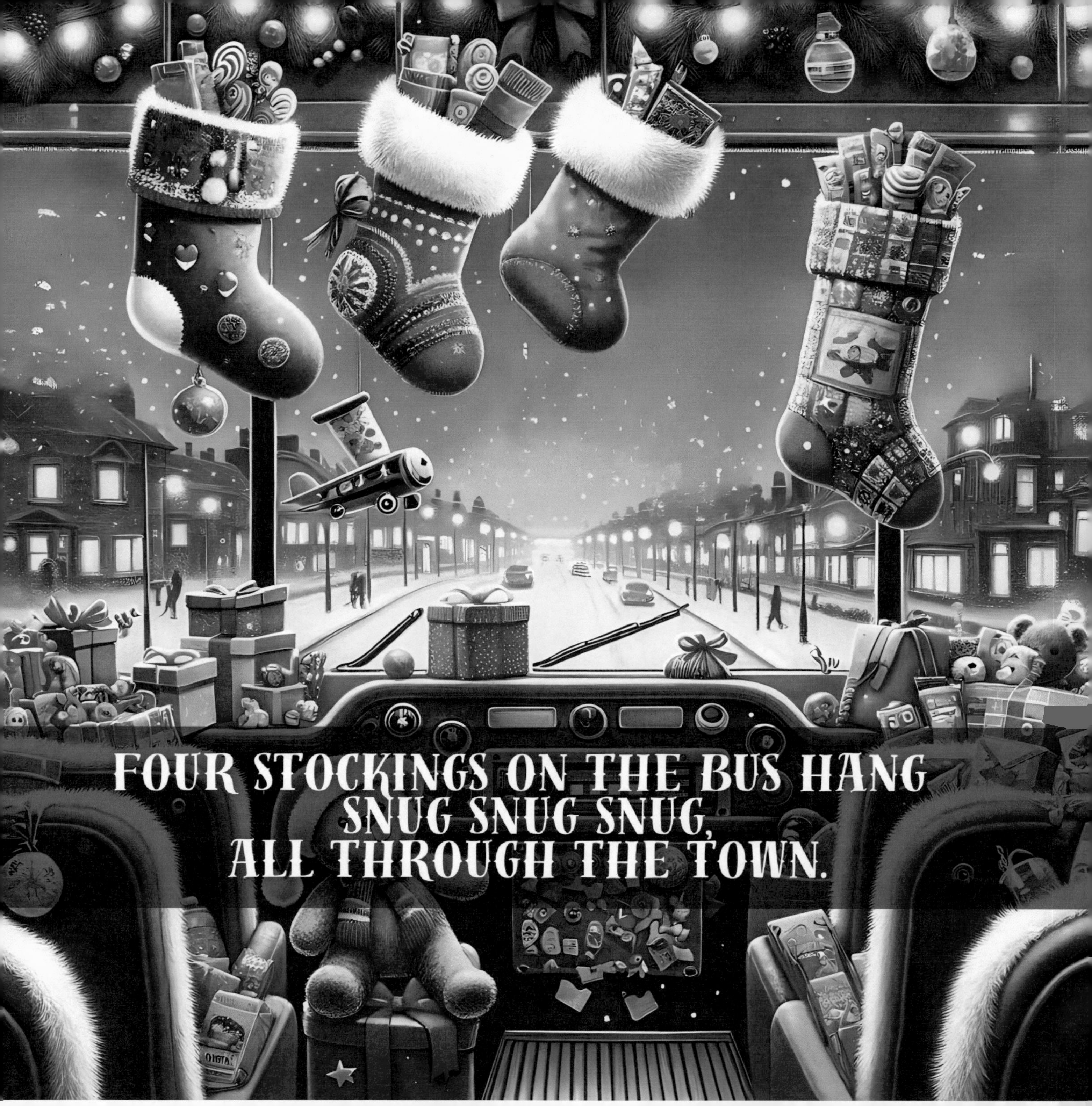
FOUR STOCKINGS ON THE BUS HANG
SNUG SNUG SNUG,
ALL THROUGH THE TOWN.

FIVE CAROLERS ON THE BUS SOUND
MERRY MERRY MERRY,
MERRY MERRY MERRY,
MERRY MERRY MERRY.

FIVE CAROLERS ON THE BUS SOUND
MERRY MERRY MERRY,
ALL THROUGH THE TOWN.

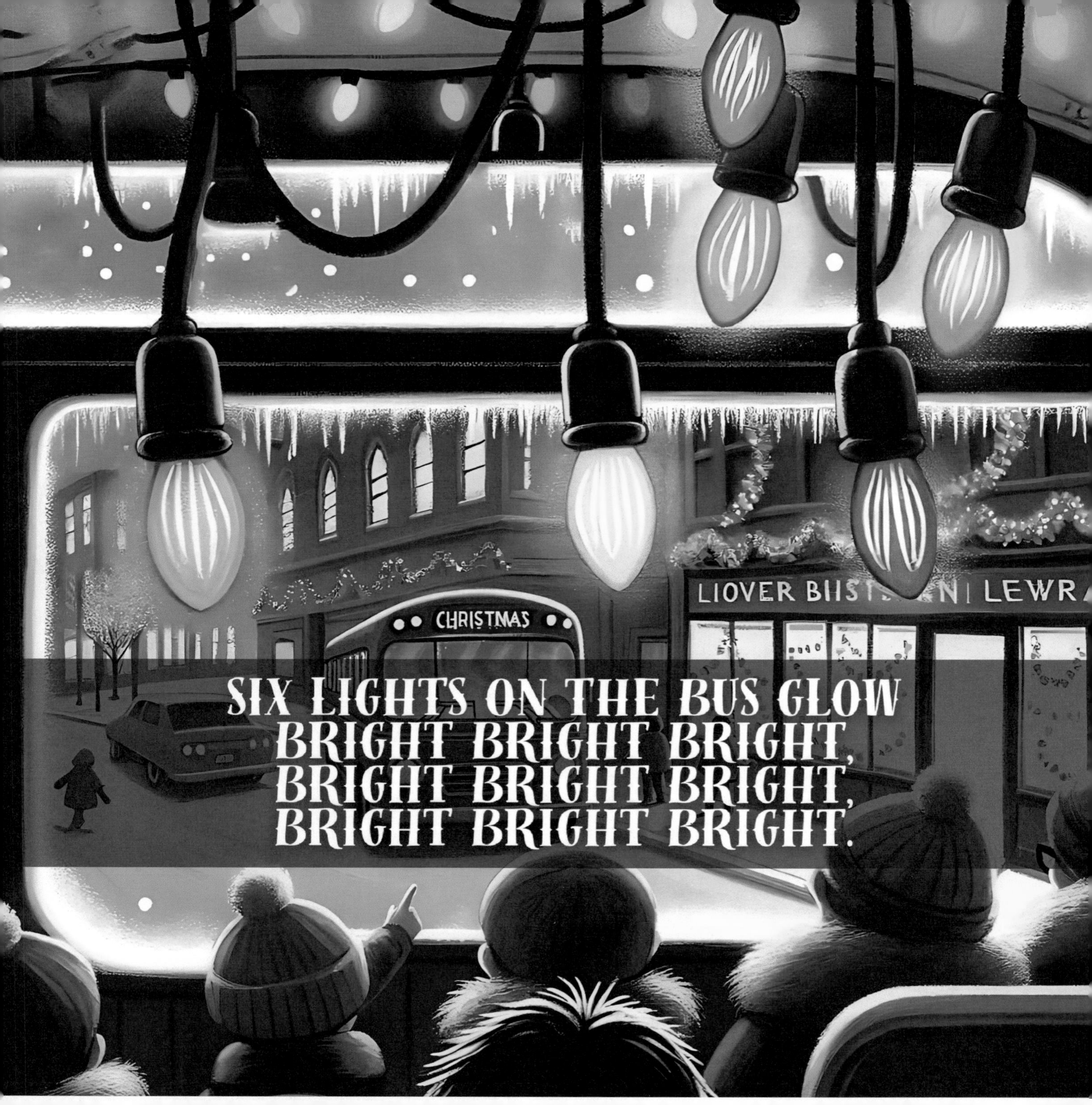


SIX LIGHTS ON THE BUS GLOW
BRIGHT BRIGHT BRIGHT,
BRIGHT BRIGHT BRIGHT,
BRIGHT BRIGHT BRIGHT.

SIX LIGHTS ON THE BUS GLOW
BRIGHT BRIGHT BRIGHT,
ALL THROUGH THE TOWN.

SEVEN COOKIES ON THE BUS TASTE
SWEET SWEET SWEET,
SWEET SWEET SWEET,
SWEET SWEET SWEET.

SEVEN COOKIES ON THE BUS TASTE
SWEET SWEET SWEET,
ALL THROUGH THE TOWN.

EIGHT SNOWFLAKES ON THE BUS FALL
SOFT SOFT SOFT,
SOFT SOFT SOFT,
SOFT SOFT SOFT.

EIGHT SNOWFLAKES ON THE BUS FALL
SOFT SOFT SOFT,
ALL THROUGH THE TOWN.

NINE GIFTS ON THE BUS BRING
JOY JOY JOY,
JOY JOY JOY,
JOY JOY JOY.

NINE GIFTS ON THE BUS BRING
JOY JOY JOY,
ALL THROUGH THE TOWN.

TEN FAMILIES ON THE BUS SHARE
LOVE AND CHEER,
LOVE AND CHEER,
LOVE AND CHEER.

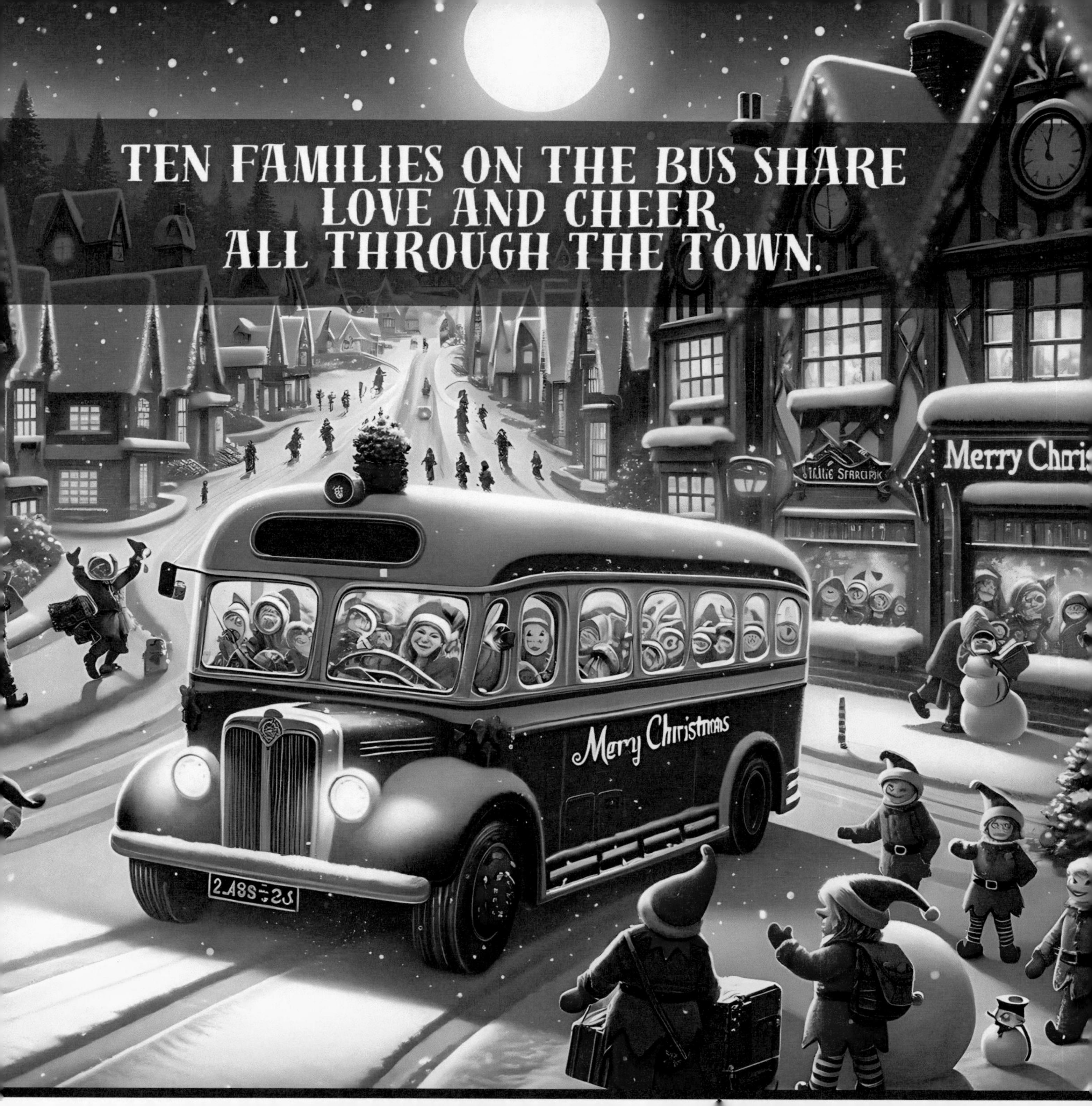


TEN FAMILIES ON THE BUS SHARE LOVE AND CHEER, ALL THROUGH THE TOWN.

ONE FESTIVE BUS GOES
JINGLE AND SHAKE,
JINGLE AND SHAKE,
JINGLE AND SHAKE.

ONE FESTIVE BUS GOES
JINGLE AND SHAKE...

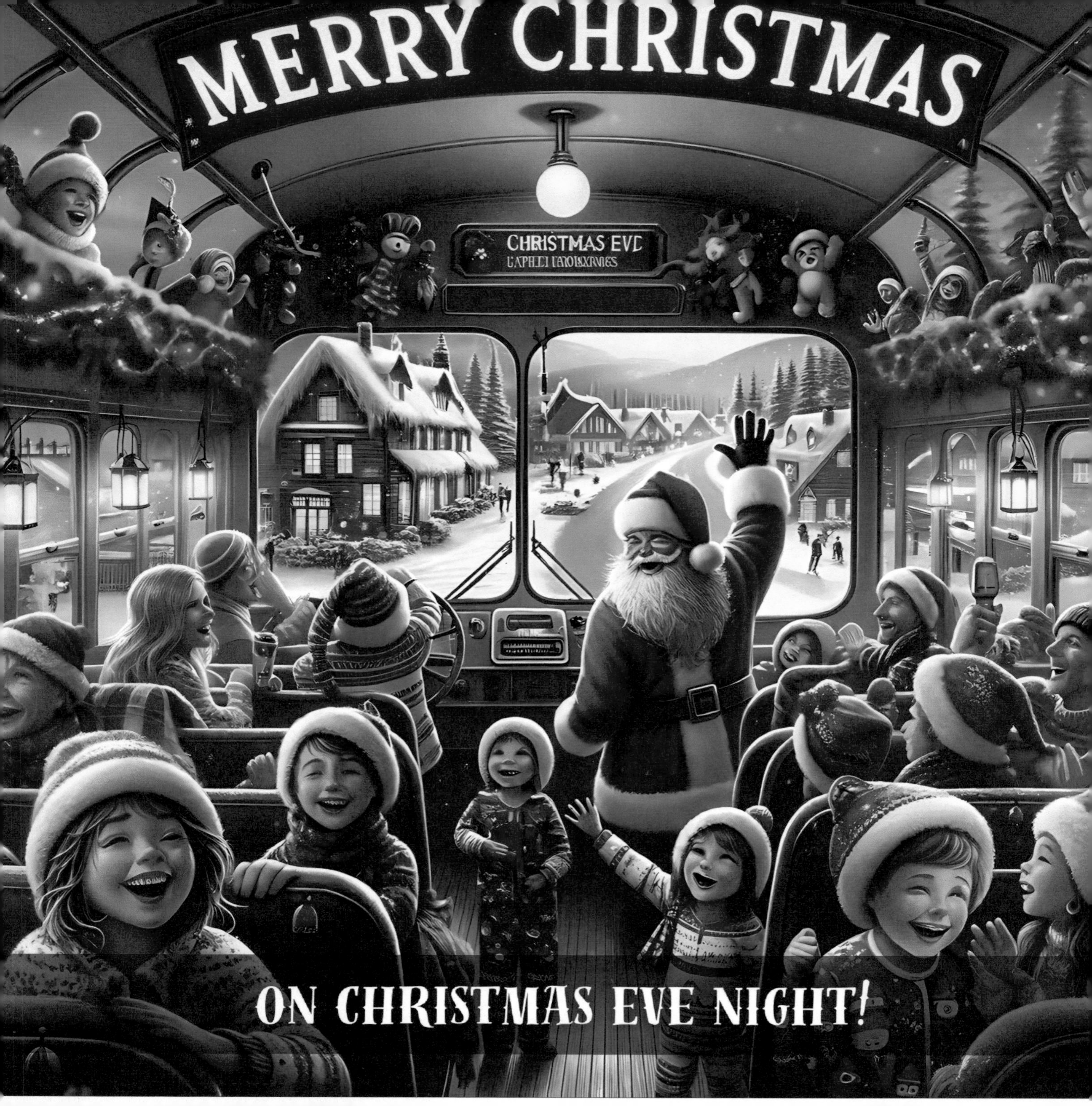
MERRY CHRISTMAS
CHRISTMAS EVD
ON CHRISTMAS EVE NIGHT!

THE END
JLC686
JINGLE AND SHAKE
33 60
ABSCO PUBLISHING

Made in United States
Cleveland, OH
01 December 2024

11157131R00017